THIS BOOK BELONGS TO

_____

PRESENTED BY

_____

OCCASION

_____

DATE

_____

PRECIOUS♡MOMENTS®

5-
MINUTE
BEDTIME
TREASURY

Tommy NELSON®

A Division of Thomas Nelson Publishers

NASHVILLE   MEXICO CITY   RIO DE JANEIRO

Precious Moments® 5-Minute Bedtime Treasury

© 2015 by Thomas Nelson
Artwork © 2015 by Precious Moments, Inc.

Published in Nashville, Tennessee, by Tommy Nelson. Tommy Nelson
is an imprint of Thomas Nelson. Thomas Nelson is a registered
trademark of HarperCollins Christian Publishing, Inc.

Licensee, Thomas Nelson. All Rights Reserved Worldwide.

Tommy Nelson titles may be purchased in bulk for educational,
business, fund-raising, or sales promotional use. For information,
please e-mail SpecialMarkets@ThomasNelson.com.

Stories retold by Jennifer Morgan Gerelds, from the
International Children's Bible®. © 1986, 1988, 1999 by Thomas
Nelson. Used by permission. All rights reserved.

ISBN-13: 978-0-7180-4319-3

Library of Congress Cataloging-in-Publication Data

Precious Moments 5-minute bedtime treasury. -- first [edition].
pages cm
ISBN 978-0-7180-4319-3 (padded hardcover) 1. Bible stories, English.
I. Precious Moments, Inc. II. Title: 5-minute bedtime treasury.
BS551.3.P74 2015
220.95'05--dc23   2015011803

Printed in China

16 17 18 LEO 10 9 8 7 6 5 4

Dedicated to John Burt,
who modeled the joy of the Lord
for children of all ages.

TABLE OF CONTENTS

Section 3: God Is Love

A COMFORTING BEDTIME ROUTINE

*B*edtime can be a stressful time of day for both parents and little ones. Between bath-time splashing, enjoying an evening snack, squirming into pajamas, and taking turns brushing teeth, the last bit of the day often feels hectic. But those last few moments before bed also can be an incredibly special time of connection for you and your children—a time when they wind down feeling secure in your love and in the love of the Creator.

As parents, we have an awesome responsibility to teach our children about God and His ways. Nurturing a love for God's Word at an early age will help boys and girls understand God's great love for them and learn to live in ways that honor Him. Deuteronomy 6:7 tells us, "Teach them to your children. Talk about them when you sit at home and walk along the road. Talk about them *when you lie down* and when you get up" (emphasis added). Bedtime is a sweet time to introduce foundational truths.

The *Precious Moments® 5-Minute Bedtime Treasury* is a Bible storybook that can help little ones learn important Bible stories in those last few quiet moments of the day. Snuggle up with your children as you read about God's mighty power and protection, the wise ways in which He guides His children, and most of all,

His great love for His people. Each story closes with a comforting Bible verse, reassuring young ones of God's love, care, and trustworthiness.

Nightly reading from the *Precious Moments® 5-Minute Bedtime Treasury* will help children wind down and create a special bedtime tradition you will cherish. But more than that, as God assures us, they will be changed as they learn stories from the Bible. Children will remember the sweet faces of beloved Precious Moments® characters and the truths that they illustrate. God's Word will be hidden in their tiny hearts, and it will grow in them and shine its light through them. Then, when they become parents themselves, they can take this same bedtime treasury, open its pastel-painted pages, and pour the love of God into their children too—continuing the rich spiritual heritage that began with a cherished bedtime ritual in your home.

The *Precious Moments® 5-Minute Bedtime Treasury* is a beautiful way to introduce your young ones to a personal relationship with God and a precious reminder of God's faithfulness that you can lovingly pass down to future generations.

FAMILY TREE

Grandmother _____

Name

_____

Birthday   Place

Grandfather _____

Name

_____

Birthday   Place

Mother _____

Name

_____

Birthday   Place

Me _____

Name

_____

Birthday   Place

_____ Grandmother
Name

_____
Birthday   Place

_____ Grandfather
Name

_____
Birthday   Place

_____ Father
Name

_____
Birthday   Place

Brothers and Sisters

_____ _____ _____
Name   Birthday   Place

_____ _____ _____
Name   Birthday   Place

_____ _____ _____
Name   Birthday   Place

_____ _____ _____
Name   Birthday   Place

ALL ABOUT ME

Name_____ Age _____

When I grow up, I want to be . . .

_____

_____

My favorite thing to do with my family is . . .

_____

_____

My best memory is . . .

_____

_____

Before I fall asleep at night, I think about . . .

_____

_____

I can't go to sleep without . . .

_____

_____

This is how big my hand is . . .

Date _____

CHURCH RECORD

Special Ceremonies

(Baptism, Dedication, Christening, First Communion, Confirmation . . .)

CEREMONY	DATE
CEREMONY	DATE
CEREMONY	DATE
CEREMONY	DATE

Church & Sunday Schools Attended

CHURCH	CITY	DATE
CHURCH	CITY	DATE
CHURCH	CITY	DATE

Vacation Bible Schools

CHURCH	CITY	DATE
CHURCH	CITY	DATE
CHURCH	CITY	DATE

Church Camps

CHURCH	CITY	DATE
CHURCH	CITY	DATE
CHURCH	CITY	DATE

GOD IS TRUSTWORTHY

Stories from the Old Testament

CREATION

Genesis 1–2

*I*n the very beginning, the earth was empty and dark. Suddenly, God said, "Let there be light!"

Bright, shining light streamed from the sky. "That's good!" God smiled. He separated the light from the darkness. Then there was day and night! It was the first day.

Next, God made air to divide the water in two. God named the air "sky."

Then God decided, "It's time for the dry land to appear!" Mountains shot up from the seas.

Beaches glistened in the sun. Rolling hills and plains stretched on for miles.

"And now for the trees and plants," God said. Then He created delicious fruit trees and towering pines. He dotted the land with shrubs and flowers, vines and vegetables. The rich rainbow of colors soaked up the light. "It's good!" God said.

Looking to the skies, God spoke again. "Shine warmly, sun! Glow brightly, moon!" And all the stars God made twinkled in the night sky.

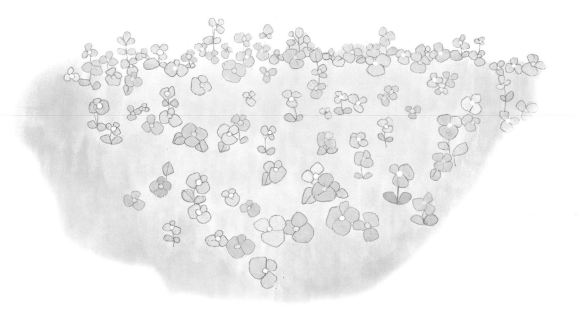

On the fifth day, God added new life! Suddenly, colorful birds appeared and flapped their wings for the first time. Then the waters on the earth began to bubble and swirl. Fish were swimming everywhere! And all the other sea creatures God made joined in the fun.

But His creation wasn't finished. "Let there be furry bunnies and fast cheetahs!" God said with delight. "Fill the land with wrinkly elephants and tall giraffes. Let the animals play on my earth!" And they did. God saw that it was good too.

Then the Lord God took dust from the ground and formed man from it. He breathed into the shape, and it moved! He was alive! "His name is Adam," God said. Then God made Eve from one of Adam's ribs. "I want you to have children and take care of My creation!" God said. Looking over all He had made, God said this time, "It's very good!"

Bedtime Bible Promise

By the seventh day God finished the work
he had been doing. So on the seventh day
he rested from all his work.
—Genesis 2:2

THE GARDEN OF EDEN

Genesis 3

A very clever snake slithered up to Eve in the garden. She didn't know it was the Devil trying to trick her.

"Did God really say that you can't eat any fruit in the garden?" the snake hissed.

"Oh, no," Eve answered. "We may eat fruit from the garden! We just can't eat or touch the fruit from the tree in the middle of the garden. If we do," she added, "God says we'll die."

"You will not die!" the snake lied. "You'll just learn about good and evil. You'll be just like God!"

Eve looked at the fruit. It was so shiny and colorful! Then she took a bite. "It's delicious! Here, Adam, you try it!" She handed it to him. Adam ate it too.

Suddenly, everything changed. "We need to put some clothes on," Adam and Eve said, as they noticed they were naked. "Let's sew some leaves for clothes." Then they heard God coming. "Let's hide!" they whispered.

"What have you done, Adam?" God asked, even though He knew they had disobeyed.

"It's Eve's fault," Adam answered. "She gave me the fruit."

"But the snake tricked me!" Eve cried.

So God punished the snake, then Eve and Adam.

It was so sad! Adam and Eve had to leave the beautiful garden. But God still loved them deeply. He clothed them with animal skins and found them a new place to live.

Bedtime Bible Promise

My mind and my body may become weak.
But God is my strength. He is mine forever.
—Psalm 73:26

NOAH AND THE ARK

Genesis 6–9

*M*any years had passed since God made the earth. People were everywhere! Sadly, the people had forgotten about God. They did whatever they wanted. They disobeyed God every day.

But Noah was different. He remembered God and loved Him with all of his heart. He obeyed God, even when no one else did.

"Noah," God said one day, "you need to build a very large boat. I'm going to save you and your family. I'll even send two of each kind of animal to put on the boat. But I'm going to destroy everything else with a flood."

Noah obeyed God right away. He followed God's directions carefully. It took a very long time to finish the boat. All the people thought Noah was being silly.

But he wasn't. When he finally finished, God brought animals of every kind to the ark. "Take your family and the animals inside," God said. Then it happened!

Splish. Splash. Fat drops of rain hit the ground. "What's this?" the people cried. But it was too late! Suddenly, rain gushed like a waterfall. Underground springs split, and water shot up, lifting the boat. Only Noah, his family, and the animals inside the ark were safe.

The rain lasted for forty days and nights. After it stopped, it took a very long time for the water to dry up. At last, land appeared. "It's time!" Noah

called out. Everyone got off the boat. God had saved them!

Noah made an offering to show God his thanks. "I'll never destroy the earth with a flood again," God said. Then God painted the sky with a beautiful rainbow as a sign of His promise.

Bedtime Bible Promise

Those who go to God Most High for safety will be protected by God All-Powerful.

—Psalm 91:1

JOSEPH SOLD INTO SLAVERY

Genesis 37

Jacob had twelve sons. Joseph, though, was his favorite. "Look, Joseph," Jacob said one day. "I have made you a beautiful robe!" Joseph loved it, but the gift made all of his brothers very jealous.

Later Joseph began to have strange dreams. He told his parents and brothers about them. "I had a dream that while we were working in the field, all your bundles of grain bowed down to mine!" In another dream, Joseph remembered seeing the sun, moon, and eleven stars. "All of them bowed down to me!" he said with excitement. But his brothers just got angrier.

One day, Jacob told Joseph to go find his brothers. They were tending sheep far from home. Joseph gladly obeyed, not knowing what his brothers had planned.

When the brothers saw Joseph coming, they whispered, "Now's our chance to get rid of that dreamer! Let's kill him!" But Reuben stopped them. "Let's just throw him in this dry well, instead."

When Joseph arrived, they tore off his robe and threw him in the well. "I know," said Judah. "Let's sell him to slave traders! Then we can make some money!" Everyone agreed. Soon they had sold Joseph to be a slave in Egypt.

Then they ruined Joseph's robe and walked home. They showed it to their father. "My son has been killed by a wild animal!" Jacob sobbed.

He didn't know that Joseph would become a successful ruler in Egypt and a faithful man who loved his God. Many years later, Joseph would forgive his brothers and save his whole family.

Bedtime Bible Promise

You, Lord, give true peace.
You give peace to those who depend on you.
You give peace to those who trust you.
—Isaiah 26:3

MOSES AND THE BASKET

Exodus 1–2

God's people had had many children and grandchildren in Egypt. Now there were so many Israelites that the king of Egypt became upset. "Look! The people of Israel are too many and too strong for us to handle!" he said. "Don't let any of their baby boys live," he ordered the Hebrew nurses.

Meanwhile, a family that loved God gave birth to a beautiful baby boy. "I don't want him to die," his mother said. So she made a basket that

could float. Then she put baby Moses inside it and gently set the basket in the Nile River. Miriam, Moses' sister, watched the basket from a distance.

Just a short time later, the basket floated near where the princess of Egypt was taking a bath. "What's that?" she asked her servant girls. "Get that basket for me." They brought it to her, and she discovered the baby inside. "Oh, he's crying!" she exclaimed. "This is one of the Hebrew babies."

Miriam had been watching everything. Quickly, she stepped forward. "I can get a Hebrew mother to nurse him for you," she offered. The princess agreed, and Miriam ran to get her mother.

So Moses grew up in the palace courts, tended by his real family and Egyptian kings and queens.

Bedtime Bible Promise

I can lie down and go to sleep. And I will
wake up again because the Lord protects me.
—Psalm 3:5

CROSSING THE RED SEA

Exodus 12–14

The people of Egypt had already seen God's anger at their sin. Nine horrible plagues had almost completely destroyed their land. During the tenth plague, the king's own firstborn son died. "Get up and leave my people!" Egypt's king ordered Moses. "Go worship God with all His people, and bless me!" Moses and the Israelites quickly gathered their belongings and left Egypt to follow God.

Moses led the huge crowd of Israelites across the dusty land. God guided them all by a cloud pillar during the day. At night, the cloud became a pillar of fire lighting their way. They were so happy to leave Egypt!

But suddenly, Egypt's king changed his mind. "What have we done? We have lost our slaves!" he roared. "Go after them!" he commanded all the soldiers in his powerful army.

By that time, Moses and God's people were camped at the Red Sea. Soon they could see Egypt's army racing toward them. "We're going to die!" they cried. But Moses said, "Don't be afraid! Stand still and see the Lord save you today!"

Then Moses lifted his staff toward the Red Sea. Instantly, the deep waters cracked and pulled apart! A dry path stretched out in front of them. All God's people crossed between the walls of water to the land on the other side.

Egypt's soldiers kept charging. Soldiers, horses, and chariots thundered onto the dry path. When all the Israelites were safely on shore, Moses held out his hand over the water. *Crash!* The walls of water smashed together and drowned the entire Egyptian army. God saved His people!

Bedtime Bible Promise

You will not fear any danger by night.
—Psalm 91:5

GOD'S COMMANDS

Exodus 19–20

Three months had passed since Israel had left Egypt. God gathered his people at the base of a very tall mountain. Then God called to Moses. "Come up here to meet with Me," He said. So Moses left the people of God and climbed Mount Sinai to talk with God.

"Tell this to the people of Israel," God instructed Moses. "Everyone has seen how I saved you from the Egyptians. So now obey Me and be My special people. You will be different from everyone else because you will belong to Me, and I will be your God."

So Moses climbed down the mountain and told the people what God had said. "We will do everything He has said," the people promised. So Moses returned to God on the mountain.

Suddenly, thunder and lightning flashed and a very thick cloud covered the top of the mountain. A loud trumpet blasted and the mountain shook wildly. The Lord was meeting with Moses!

"I am the Lord your God. Do not worship fake gods. Only worship Me," God commanded. "Do not make any idols, and do not disrespect My name by saying it without thinking," He continued.

"Remember that the Sabbath is a day of rest. Don't tell lies about your neighbor. Be happy with what you have, and don't be jealous of other people's things."

So Moses explained to them all that God had commanded.

Bedtime Bible Promise

Surely you know. Surely you have heard. The Lord is the God who lives forever. He created all the world. He does not become tired or need to rest. No one can understand how great his wisdom is.

—Isaiah 40:28

THE PEOPLE'S SIN

Exodus 31–32

God wanted His people to be different! Since they belonged to God, He wanted them to be perfect like Him. He also wanted to meet with them. So He told them how to build a special tent called the Tent of Meeting. He would meet with the priests there to tell them what He wanted the people to know.

Then God wrote His rules down on two stone tablets. He gave them to Moses. But then something bad happened while Moses was on the mountain with God.

"Go down from this mountain," God suddenly told Moses. "Your people are doing very evil things!"

Moses quickly climbed down the mountain with Joshua, his helper. Together, they heard the noise of a great big party. Then they found out why the people were celebrating.

While Moses was away, the people had gotten tired of waiting. "Aaron, we don't know what happened to Moses, so make us gods who will lead us!" they insisted. Aaron agreed, and gathered their gold jewelry. Then he melted it and shaped the gold into the form of a calf. The people loved it!

They danced wildly and worshiped the idol. They broke all of God's commands.

When Moses saw it, he was so angry! He threw his stone tablets on the ground and shattered them. Then he melted the idol, crushed it to powder, put it in water, and made the Israelites drink it.

The next day, Moses told the people, "You have sinned terribly. But now I will go to the Lord and ask Him to forgive you."

God forgave the people, even though they were in trouble. God loved them no matter what, but they had a lot to learn.

Bedtime Bible Promise

God says, "Be still and know that I am God."
—Psalm 46:10

WE WILL SERVE THE LORD

Joshua 24:1–15

Joshua had an important message from God for the people of Israel. Each of the twelve tribes sent a leader to the city of Shechem to hear what God had to say.

"A long time ago, your ancestors worshiped fake gods," God said through Joshua. "But I, the Lord, took Abraham out of that land and I led him to Canaan. I gave Abraham many children through his son Isaac. Over time, his large family became slaves in Israel.

"I chose Moses and Aaron to free you from the Egyptians. When I brought you out of Egypt, their soldiers chased My people on chariots. When Israel cried out for help, I parted the sea so they could walk through safely. But when the Egyptians passed through, I covered their army with water.

"Then I brought you to the land I wanted to give you. I drove out the bad people who lived there to make room for you."

Then Joshua said, "Now you have heard from the Lord. You need to serve Him with all of your heart. Today you must decide who you will serve," he said. "You can serve the same fake gods that our ancestors and these people here worship if you want. But as for me and my family, we will serve the Lord!"

Everyone in Israel agreed with Joshua. "We will never stop following the Lord!" they said.

Bedtime Bible Promise

The Lord gives sleep to those he loves.
—Psalm 127:2

DAVID AND GOLIATH

1 Samuel 17

The powerful Philistine army lined the hill. The Israelite army lined up on another hill, facing the Philistines. Only a small valley separated the soldiers. Every day the Philistines sent their very best soldier named Goliath to make fun of the Israelites. He was nine-foot-four-inches tall, he carried very heavy armor and a spear, and he made fun of Israel's God. "Send someone to fight me!" he ordered. "If he can fight and kill me, we will become your servants. But if I defeat and kill him, you will become our servants!" All the Israelites were afraid. No one wanted to fight Goliath.

Meanwhile, in the city of Bethlehem, a young boy named David was taking care of his sheep. Jesse, his father, sent him to check on his brothers who were in the army.

When David arrived at the camp, he heard Goliath. "Why does he think he can say bad things about our God?" David demanded to know. "I will go and fight this Philistine!" David said. He knew God would take care of him.

King Saul heard about David and sent for him. "You can't fight that mean soldier! You're only a boy. Goliath is a mighty warrior!"

David answered, "The Lord will fight for me!" Instead of the king's armor, David chose five smooth stones from a stream and a sling. Then he went to meet Goliath.

Goliath saw David coming. The giant soldier began making fun of David too. But David

shouted back, "You come to me using a sword and spear. But I come to you in the name of the Lord!"

Then David ran fast toward Goliath and flung a rock from his sling. The stone sank deeply into Goliath's forehead and he fell down dead. Israel's army cheered in triumph and chased the Philistine army away.

Bedtime Bible Promise

I will say to the Lord, "You are my place of safety and protection. You are my God, and I trust you."
—Psalm 91:2

DANIEL IN THE LIONS' DEN

Daniel 6:4–23

King Darius loved Daniel because he was a good servant who always did what was right. Daniel also loved God. But Darius's other leaders hated Daniel. They wanted to get rid of him. So Daniel's enemies came up with a plan to trick the king into killing Daniel.

"King Darius, live forever!" they said as they came before his throne. "All of your wise leaders have agreed that you should order a new law," they said. "For the next 30 days, no one should pray to any god or man except you. Anyone who doesn't obey will be thrown into the lions' den!"

So King Darius wrote the new law. Daniel heard about it, but he didn't obey the king. He obeyed God instead. Daniel kept right on praying to God every day, by his window, just like always.

It wasn't hard for Daniel's enemies to catch him. They found him in his upstairs room praying in front of the open windows. They brought him before King Darius.

"King Darius, Daniel is not obeying you. He still prays to his God three times every day," they reported. King Darius became very upset. *Isn't there some way to save Daniel?* he wondered. But the law had already been written.

So the soldiers threw Daniel into the lions' den. King Darius cried, "May the God you serve all the time save you!"

Early the next morning, King Darius hurried back to the lions' den and called out, "Daniel, servant of the living God! Has your God been able to save you from the lions?"

Daniel answered, "My God sent His angel to close the lions' mouths. They have not hurt me!"

Darius was so happy! He quickly freed Daniel. Then he threw his enemies into the den of lions.

Bedtime Bible Promise

"I told you these things so that you can have peace in me. In this world you will have trouble. But be brave! I have defeated the world!"
—John 16:33

JONAH RUNS FROM GOD

Jonah 1:1– 2:10

*L*ong ago, the Lord spoke to Jonah. He said, "I want you to travel to the great city of Nineveh. The people there do many bad things and I want you to preach against it."

But Jonah ran away from the Lord and went to the city of Joppa instead. He found a ship going to a city called Tarshish. He paid the crew to let him ride on the ship, thinking he could escape the Lord.

But the Lord sent a storm on the sea and made it very rough. The ship was in danger of breaking apart. All the sailors were afraid it would sink, so they started throwing things off to make the boat lighter. They prayed to their gods for help.

Jonah was asleep on the ship when the captain came and said, "Why are you sleeping? Get up and pray to your God so maybe He will save us!"

Then all the sailors threw lots to find out who was causing the troubles they were having on the sea. It was determined that their trouble had come because of Jonah. "I know it's my fault that the storm has come upon us," Jonah said. "Throw me into the sea; then the waters will calm down." So the men picked him up and threw him into the sea. Suddenly, the water became calm. All the men on the boat feared Jonah's God even more.

Then the Lord caused a very big fish to swallow Jonah to keep him safe. Jonah stayed three days and three nights in the fish's huge stomach. While he was there, he prayed to the Lord his God. Jonah said:

"I was in danger, so I called to You and You answered. I was about to die, and You heard me and saved me. You threw me into the sea, and the waters were all around me. But You saved me from death! Lord, I praise You and thank You! Thank You for saving me! I will keep all my promises to You, Lord."

Then the Lord spoke to the big fish. The fish spit Jonah out onto the dry land! After God saved him, Jonah went to Ninevah as God had asked him to do.

Bedtime Bible Promise

You won't need to be afraid when you lie down.
When you lie down, your sleep will be peaceful.
—Proverbs 3:24

GOD IS GOOD

Words of Praise and Wisdom

YOUR NAME IS WONDERFUL

Psalm 8:1–8

*L*ord, You are our Master! Your name is the most wonderful of all! The heavens shout Your praise. You have taught children and even babies to sing about how great You are!

I look at the heavens, which You made with Your hands. I see the moon and stars, which You created. They seem so big and important, but we are so small.

Why are people important to You? Why do You take care of us?

Though we are small, You have made us very special. You put Your people in charge of everything You made! Your people rule over all the fluffy sheep and grazing cows, all the powerful lions and strong bears. You've put us in charge of all the majestic eagles and colorful parrots, and even the mighty sharks and whales! Our power comes from You, and You rule over us.

Lord our Master, Your name is the most wonderful name in all the earth!

Bedtime Bible Promise

For anyone who enters and has God's rest will rest from his work as God did.
—Hebrews 4:10

THE LORD TAKES CARE OF HIS PEOPLE

Psalm 16:1–9, 11

Protect me, God, because I trust in You. I said to the Lord, "You are my Lord. Every good thing I have comes from You."

I love to be with other people who serve and love You, God. But some people have turned from You. They worship fake idols. I will never follow them.

No, the Lord is all I need. You take care of me. You have made my life beautiful.

Praise Your name, Lord! You guide me through the day; even at night You keep on leading me. I will always keep You in front of me so that I know where to go. I will not be hurt. So I'm happy, and I am glad! Even my body has hope.

You will teach me God's way to live. Being with You fills me with so much joy! Being right beside You brings me more happiness than anything else.

Bedtime Bible Promise

He who guards you never sleeps.
—Psalm 121:3

THE LORD IS MY SHEPHERD

Psalm 23:1–6

The Lord is my shepherd. He gives me everything I need! When I'm tired, He takes me to beautiful, green grass for rest. He takes me to drink from cool, calm waters. He gives me strength for the day. Because He is good, He leads me on the right paths.

Even if I walk through a very dark valley, I will not be afraid because You are with me. You protect me with Your shepherd's rod and staff.

You prepare a meal for me in front of my enemies. They see how good You are to me. You pour oil on my head. You give me more than I can hold. I can never outlive Your goodness and love to me. And I will live in the Lord's house forever!

Bedtime Bible Promise

He gives me rest in green pastures.

—Psalm 23:2

TELLING THE TRUTH

Psalm 32:1–11

When God forgives our sin, we are so happy! What a blessing that God can take our guilt away! When we are forgiven, we are perfect before God.

But sometimes I've tried to hide my sin. It made me feel weak deep inside me. I worried all day long. My strength was gone as in the summer heat.

Then I told God what I did wrong. I quit hiding my sin, and I turned to the Lord. I said, "I will confess my sins to the Lord." And He forgave me!

We should all pray to You right away, while there is time. When troubles rise like a flood, I will not get hurt. I hide in You because You protect me. You fill me with happy songs about how You saved me.

The Lord says, "I will make you wise. I will show you where to go. I will guide you and watch over you. Don't be like a horse or donkey. They don't understand. They must be led with bits and reins, or they will not come near you."

People who turn from God run into a lot of trouble, but the Lord's love covers those who trust Him. Everyone, sing and be happy in the Lord!

Bedtime Bible Promise

Lord, you are kind and forgiving. You have great love for those who call to you.

—Psalm 86:5

WISHING TO BE NEAR GOD

Psalm 63:1–8

God, You are my God. I want to follow You! I am like a person who travels in a hot, dry desert. I am so thirsty for You!

I have seen You with my own eyes in Your beautiful Temple. You are so strong and full of glory! Your love is better than anything else in life. I will tell how great You are as long as I live! When I pray to You, I will lift up my hands. I know good will come from You. I will be full of Your goodness, as if I had just eaten the very best meal. I will use the mouth You gave me to sing praises to You.

While I'm lying in bed, I remember You and
think about You through the night. You help me!
Because You protect me, I sing with joy. Your
strong hand supports me, so I will always stay by
Your side!

Bedtime Bible Promise

"I say this because I know what I have planned for you," says the Lord. "I have good plans for you. I don't plan to hurt you. I plan to give you hope and a good future."

—Jeremiah 29:11

LORD, TEACH ME YOUR RULES

Psalm 119:1–2, 9–20, 24

People who live pure lives and keep God's rules are the happiest of all. They follow the Lord and ask Him for help!

How can children live lives that make God happy? We can do it by obeying God's Word! God, I want to obey You with my whole heart. Please help me to do what's right. I have put Your words in my heart so that I won't forget them and sin against You.

Lord, You should be praised. Teach me what You want. Then I'll tell other people about all Your right ways. I enjoy living by Your rules as much as some people enjoy a lot of money. I think about Your orders and study Your ways. Because I enjoy Your words so much, I will not forget them.

Please open my eyes so that I can see how wonderful Your teachings truly are! This earth is not my home. I want to study and know Your ways. Please don't hide them from me!

I delight in Your rules. They're the best teachings for my life!

Bedtime Bible Promise

The Lord says, "I will make you wise.
I will show you where to go. I will guide
you and watch over you."
—Psalm 32:8

THE WORD OF GOD

Psalm 119

You created me with Your own hands, so You can help me understand You. Teach me so that I can learn Your ways.

I love to serve You. You promised to comfort me with Your love. Please show kindness to me so that I may live a good life. How I love Your teachings!

Lord, Your word never ends! It stays true forever in heaven. You never

stop being friends with Your people. You made the earth, and it still stands.

Your word lights my way like a bright and shining lamp.

I will follow Your rules forever. They make me happy! I will try to always do what You have asked for as long as I live.

You protect me like a shield, so I hide myself in You.

Help me, and I will be saved. I will always respect Your rules.

I love Your commands more than the purest gold.

PROTECTION AND GUIDANCE

Psalm 121:1–8

The hills do not protect me. So where does my help come from? It comes from the Lord! He made heaven and earth.

He will not let you be defeated. The Lord always guards you. He never sleeps or even rests! The Lord protects you as the shade protects you from the sun. The sun cannot hurt you during the day. And the moon cannot hurt you at night.

The Lord will guard your life from all dangers. He will protect you in all that you do—both now and forever.

Bedtime Bible Promise

I go to bed and sleep in peace.
Lord, only you keep me safe.
—Psalm 4:8

PRAISE THE LORD

Psalm 150:1–6

Praise the Lord!

Praise God in His Temple. Worship Him in His mighty heaven. How strong and great is our God!

Sound the trumpets. Pluck the harps and lyres. Dance and shake the tambourine. Play the flute. Fill the air with the sound of stringed instruments. Praise Him with loud, crashing cymbals. Let everything that breathes praise the Lord!

Praise the Lord!

Bedtime Bible Promise

....

Give thanks to the God of heaven.

His love continues forever.

—Psalm 136:26

THE WISE WORDS OF SOLOMON

Proverbs 1:1–9, 15

David's son, Solomon, became Israel's king. These are his wise words:

The smart person listens to words of wisdom. By them, you learn how to obey and understand God's rules. They teach you what is honest, fair, and right. They help you to think the right way, even if you don't know everything. Smart people listen to them and keep on learning.

They learn how to understand the words and
riddles of wise men.

Being wise starts with loving and obeying the Lord.
Only foolish people hate following His ways.

My child, listen to what your mother and father teach you. Their instruction will make your life beautiful, like a gold necklace or fragrant flowers in your hair.

Do not follow sinners who tell you to go the wrong way. Do not do what they do!

Bedtime Bible Promise

Your word is like a lamp for my feet
and a light for my way.
—Psalm 119:105

THE REWARDS OF WISDOM

Proverbs 2:1–12

My child, believe and remember what I say! Listen to my wise words. Do everything you can to understand. Call out to God for wisdom. Beg for understanding. Search for it like a hidden treasure. When you do, you will start to understand how great the Lord is.

As you learn respect, you will begin to know God. Only the Lord gives wisdom and understanding. He gladly gives it to those who are honest. Like a shield He protects the people who haven't done wrong and those who stay close friends with God.

Then you will understand what is honest and fair and right. You'll know what to do. Your good sense will protect you and keep you from doing evil. It will save you from people who speak lies.

Bedtime Bible Promise

We know that in everything God works for the good of those who love him. They are the people God called, because that was his plan.
—Romans 8:28

REMEMBER THE LORD

Proverbs 3:1–8

*M*y child, don't forget my teaching. Keep thinking about what I've said. Then you'll live a long time and your life will be very good.

Don't ever stop being kind and truthful. Let truth and kindness fill everything you do. Write them on your mind like a list on a piece of paper. Then others will think well of you, and God will be happy.

Trust the Lord with all of your heart. Even if it doesn't make sense to you, trust God's words

anyway. Remember the Lord in everything you do, and He will tell you where to go.

Don't do what you think is smart. Trust God instead, and do what He tells you. Then you will have a healthy body and strong bones.

Bedtime Bible Promise

Those who know the Lord trust him. He will not leave those who come to him.

—Psalm 9:10

TRAIN UP A CHILD

Proverbs 22:1–4, 6

*I*t is better to be known for your goodness than it is to have a lot of money. It's better for people to think well of you than to own many things.

Rich people and poor people are really the same. God made them all!

When wise people see danger coming, they get out of the way. Foolish people keep going and get into trouble.

Don't be proud. Respect the Lord and He will bring you all that you need in life.

Teach children how to live God's way when they are young. As they grow up, they will remember what they learned. They will continue to follow God.

Bedtime Bible Promise

[Jesus] said to them, "Let the little children come to me. Don't stop them. The kingdom of God belongs to people who are like these little children."

—Mark 10:14

A TIME FOR EVERYTHING

Ecclesiastes 3:1–8

*T*here is a right time for everything. Everything on earth has its special season. Every day someone is born and someone dies. We plant in the right season, and clear the fields after the food has been picked. At times, we hunt for food. At other times, we help heal those who are hurt. Sometimes we must tear things down before we can build something stronger and better.

Sometimes it is best to cry. But laughing at the right time can be just what is needed.

It is okay to be sad sometimes. When you are happy, it's time to celebrate! There is a time to throw away stones and a time to gather them. Hug someone when the time is right. But don't hug them longer than they want.

Search hard when you lose something, but know when it's time to give up looking. Keep a few special things, but learn to give some things away. Sometimes it's best to rip things apart. At other times, sew them together.

Be silent when you need to listen. Then speak when the time is right. It is always time to love what is good. Always hate what is evil. Sometimes countries are at war, but in the end, God brings peace.

Bedtime Bible Promise

Give all your worries to him,
because he cares for you.
—1 Peter 5:7

FRIENDS AND FAMILY GIVE STRENGTH

Ecclesiastes 4:9–12

*I*t is much easier to get work done when two people work together. If one person falls and gets hurt, the other person can help him get up. But if he is alone when he falls, no one can help him. It is easier to keep warm when two people are together. When you're all alone, it's hard to stay warm in the cold.

An enemy might be able to hurt someone who is alone. But when people come together, they can protect themselves. A rope made of three strands wrapped together is strong. It's very hard to break.

Bedtime Bible Promise

As for me and my family, we will serve the Lord.
—Joshua 24:15

THE KING OF PEACE IS COMING

Isaiah 11:1–7, 9–10

A new king is coming from Jesse's family. He will grow like a branch that sprouts from an old stump. God's Spirit will fill this king and give Him the power to know and obey God perfectly. He will lead God's people in the right way. The Spirit will teach Him to know and respect the Lord. He will gladly obey what God says. He will not judge other people by what they look like on the outside.

He will always do what's right. With a word He will destroy evil people, and He will rule with goodness and right judgment.

Even wild animals will grow tame. Wolves will rest with sheep, and leopards will lie calmly with goats. All the animals will eat together in peace. And a little child will lead them.

No one will hurt another anymore because all of creation will know God.

Then the king from Jesse's family will draw people to His home. The place where He lives will shine with His glory!

Bedtime Bible Promise

"All people will know that you are my followers
if you love each other."
—John 13:35

GOD IS LOVE

Stories from the New Testament

JESUS' BIRTH AND THE WISE MEN'S VISIT

Matthew 1:18–24; 2:1–12

Mary was planning to marry Joseph. Suddenly, an angel appeared in her house!

"Don't be afraid, Mary, because God is pleased with you!" the angel said. Then he told her that she was going to have a baby. "It will be God's own Son, born through the power of the Holy Spirit," he said.

Surprised, Mary answered, "I am the Lord's servant. Let this happen to me as you say!" Then the angel left.

At first, Joseph was upset when Mary told him the news. But God sent an angel at night to explain God's plan to Joseph. So they married and traveled to Bethlehem, where she gave birth to Jesus.

A short time later, wise men from the east journeyed to Jerusalem to find the special baby. They came to King Herod first and asked, "Where is the baby who was born to be the king of the Jews? We saw His star in the east," they explained. "We came to worship Him."

News of a new king bothered King Herod. He told the wise men, "Go and look carefully to find the child. When you find Him, come tell me so I can worship Him too." Secretly Herod planned to kill the new king.

The star continued to lead the wise men straight to Jesus in Bethlehem. When they found Him, they were so happy! Bowing before Jesus, they brought Him treasures of gold, frankincense, and myrrh.

But God warned them not to return to Herod. So the wise men went home another way.

Bedtime Bible Promise

Everyone who believes that Jesus is
the Christ is God's child.
—1 John 5:1

JESUS VISITS THE TEMPLE

Luke 2:41–51

Every year Jesus' parents went to Jerusalem for the Passover Feast. When Jesus was twelve years old, they went to the feast as they always did. When it was over, they started toward home.

After traveling a full day, Mary asked Joseph, "Where is Jesus?" They began to ask friends and relatives. "We haven't seen Him," they all said. Mary and Joseph were worried. "We must go back to Jerusalem and look for Him there," they decided.

Mary and Joseph searched Jerusalem for three days. At last, they found Jesus in the Temple talking with the priests and teachers. He was asking them questions and listening to them. "This boy has amazing understanding and wise answers!" the leaders said.

"Son, why did You do this to us?" Mary asked Jesus. "Your father and I were very worried about You. We have been looking for You!"

Jesus answered, "Why did you have to look for Me? You should have known that I must be where My Father's work is!" Mary and Joseph did not understand what Jesus meant, but they were very happy to find Him. "Let's go home now," they said. Jesus gladly obeyed.

At home, Jesus continued to learn more and more and to grow bigger and stronger. People liked Him, and He pleased God.

Bedtime Bible Promise

You are young, but do not let anyone treat you as
if you were not important. Be an example to show
the believers how they should live. Show them
with your words, with the way you live, with your
love, with your faith, and with your pure life.

—1 Timothy 4:12

THE LIGHT OF THE WORLD

John 3

*I*t was nighttime when Nicodemus came to Jesus. As a Pharisee, he was an important Jewish leader. But he wanted to hear more about what Jesus had to say.

Jesus told him, "I tell you the truth. Unless one is born again, he cannot be in God's kingdom."

Nicodemus was very confused. "How can anyone be born twice?" he asked. So Jesus explained, "He must be born from water and the Spirit." Then Jesus taught Nicodemus about how all the Scriptures told of Jesus' coming. "The Son of Man must be lifted up on a cross, just like Moses lifted up the snake on the pole in the desert and saved the people," Jesus said. "God loved the world so much that He sent His only Son. Whoever believes in Him will not be lost, but will have eternal life."

Then Jesus explained to Nicodemus why some people would not believe Him. "I am the Light from God that has come into the world. But some people did not want the light," Jesus told him. "They wanted darkness because the light showed all their bad deeds. But the person who follows the true way loves the light."

Bedtime Bible Promise

"In the same way, you should be a light for other people. Live so that they will see the good things you do. Live so that they will praise your Father in heaven."
—Matthew 5:16

JESUS TEACHES THE PEOPLE

Matthew 6:7–21, 25, 33

*J*esus explained to the people what obedience to God looks like. "Don't be like those people who don't know God but pray to Him anyway. They may use big words and sound important, but they don't mean anything," Jesus warned them. "Your Father knows what you need before you even ask Him. So when you pray, say:

'Father in heaven, Your name is perfect. Please set up Your kingdom here on earth like You have in

heaven. Give us the food we need each day and forgive us for our sins. We will forgive people who hurt us too. Do not cause us to be tested, but protect us from the Evil One.'"

Then Jesus showed the difference between people who pretend to know God and real believers. "Don't try to get people to notice you when you fast or pray. Keep it a secret between you and God, and He will reward you. Remember that heavenly treasures are worth a lot more than anything on earth. Moths, rust, and thieves ruin things here, but heavenly riches last forever."

Then Jesus taught them about trust. "Don't worry and say, 'What will we eat?' or 'What will we drink?' or 'What will we wear?' All the people who don't know God worry about these things. But your Father knows what you need, and He will take care of you," Jesus reminded them. "What you should want most is God's kingdom and doing what God wants. He'll give you everything else you need."

Bedtime Bible Promise

Do not worry about anything. But pray
and ask God for everything you need.
And when you pray, always give thanks.

—Philippians 4:6

SERMON ON THE HILL

Matthew 5

Crowds of people followed Jesus. They all wanted to hear what He had to say. So He went up on a hill with His followers to teach them. He said:

"Everyone who knows they need God is happy because the kingdom of heaven belongs to them.

"Those who are sad are happy because God will comfort them.

"Those who are humble are happy because the earth will belong to them.

"Those who really want to do right are happy because God will give them everything they need.

"Those who show kindness to others are happy because kindness will be given them.

"Those who are pure in their thinking are happy because they will be with God.

"Those who work to bring peace are happy. God will call them His sons.

"And those who are treated badly for doing good are happy because the kingdom of heaven belongs to them."

Then Jesus explained that people will say bad things about His followers. "They will lie and say evil things because you follow Me," Jesus warned. "But when they do, rejoice and be glad! You have a great reward waiting for you in heaven."

Then Jesus taught His people that they are the salt of the earth and the light to the world.

"Live so that others will see the good things you do. Live so that they will praise your Father in heaven," Jesus encouraged them.

Bedtime Bible Promise

The Lord shows mercy and is kind. He does not become angry quickly, and he has great love.
—Psalm 103:8

THE STORY ABOUT PLANTING SEED

Matthew 13:3–8, 19–23

Jesus often used stories to help the people understand heavenly ideas. Once He told a story about a man who went out to plant some seed.

Some seeds fell by the road, but they were quickly eaten by birds. Some fell on rocky ground and grew into plants quickly. But their roots were short, and the plants withered in the hot sun. Some seeds fell among weeds. Though they grew, they were soon choked out by the weeds. At last, the rest of the seeds fell on good ground. They grew strong and tall and produced a large crop.

"So listen to the meaning of that story about the farmer," Jesus said. "The seed that fell by the road is like someone who hears God's Word but doesn't understand it. Then the Evil One comes and takes it away. The seed that fell on rocky ground is like someone who listens to God at first and is happy about it. But when hard times come, he stops believing God. The seed that fell among the thorny weeds is like a person who hears the teaching at first. But soon he lets the problems in this life and the love of money stop that truth from growing. But the seed that fell on good ground is like the person who hears God's words and understands them. He grows to become strong in Jesus and produces fruit."

Bedtime Bible Promise

But the Spirit gives love, joy, peace,
patience, kindness, goodness, faithfulness,
gentleness, self-control. There is no law that
says these things are wrong.

—Galatians 5:22-23

JESUS FEEDS THE 5,000 AND WALKS ON WATER

Matthew 14

All day, Jesus taught the people and healed the sick. At last, it was time for dinner. Everybody was hungry. "Send the people to town so they can buy some food," Jesus' followers said.

But Jesus answered, "You give them some food to eat."

"But we don't have enough food!" they argued. "We have only five loaves of bread and two fish."

Jesus told everybody to sit down. Then He took what little food they had and prayed. "Thank You, Father, for this food," He said. Then He put the food into baskets and had His followers pass them around. Women and children, along with 5,000 men, sat on the ground, and they all took what they needed.

Soon, everyone said, "I'm full!" When the followers gathered the baskets, they found twelve still filled with leftover food!

After dinner, it was time to go. Jesus sent His followers ahead of Him by boat.

During the night, a strong wind blew over the lake and kicked up very high waves. Suddenly, the followers saw a man walking on the water! "It's a ghost!" they cried.

But Jesus said, "It is I! Don't be afraid."

Peter answered, "If it's You, tell me to come to You on the water."

"Come," Jesus welcomed him.

Peter hopped out of the boat and walked on the water to Jesus. But when he saw the wind and waves, he became afraid and started to sink. "Lord, save me!" Peter cried. Jesus grabbed Peter and brought him to the boat.

"Your faith is small," Jesus gently corrected him. "Why did you stop believing?"

Then the wind and waves grew calm.

Bedtime Bible Promise

"Remember that I commanded you to be strong and brave. So don't be afraid. The Lord your God will be with you everywhere you go."
—Joshua 1:9

JESUS HEALS AND TEACHES

Luke 13:10–17; 15:1–7

*J*esus loved to teach and to help people.

One day He was teaching in the synagogue. A synagogue is similar to a church where people go to worship and learn. There was a woman there who was crippled. Her back was bent, and she could not stand up straight. When Jesus saw her, He said, "Woman, stand up. Your sickness has left you!" He put His hands on her, and instantly she could stand. She was so happy that she began praising God.

But the leader of the synagogue was angry because Jesus had healed her on the Sabbath day. (In those days you were not supposed to do any work on the seventh day, or the Sabbath day.)

Jesus told the synagogue leader that he was being unfair, and he was wrong. Jesus explained, "You untie your work animals and lead them to drink water every day, even on the Sabbath. This woman whom I healed is our Jewish sister. Surely it is not wrong to heal her on a Sabbath day!" When Jesus said this, all the men who were criticizing Him were ashamed. All the other people were happy for the wonderful things Jesus was doing.

Another time Jesus told a story to some teachers and other people who were watching and listening to Him. He said, "What if a man had 100 sheep, and one of them wandered off and got lost? That man would leave all the other 99 sheep to go look for his one lost sheep. He would search until he found it. Then when he finally found it, he would be so happy! He would pick up the sheep and carry it home. He would tell his friends and neighbors so they could be happy that he found his lost sheep too. I tell you that it is the same way in heaven when one sinner has a change of heart. There is so much happiness and rejoicing that one lost sinner has come to God!"

Bedtime Bible Promise

The Lord's love never ends. His mercies never stop.
—Lamentations 3:22

A SON COMES HOME

Luke 15:11–32

*J*esus told the story of a man who had two sons. The younger son wanted fun and adventure, so he asked his father for his share of the property. The father divided up the property between his two sons. The younger son took all that was his and left home. He traveled far away to another country. He was foolish and wasted all his money on things that were not good for him. Before he knew it, he had spent all his money.

Then the land got very dry. There was no rain and all the crops died. There was no food to eat. The son was so hungry! He needed money to buy food. But he had wasted all the money he had. So he got a job feeding pigs. He was so hungry that he was even willing to eat the same food the pigs had to eat. But still no one would give him anything.

So he decided that he would just go home and tell his father that he was sorry. Maybe his dad would let him at least be a servant. The servants had enough food to eat. *I will go home and apologize,* he thought.

While the son was still a long way from the house, his father saw him coming. He felt sorry for his son. The father ran to him with wide-open arms. He hugged him and kissed him and held him tight. Then the father wanted to have a feast to celebrate his son's homecoming. He told the servants to bring food and gifts for the party. "My son was dead, but now he is alive again! He was lost, but now he is found!" So they all began to celebrate.

But the older son was still in the field. When he came home, he saw the party and asked one of his father's servants, "What's going on here? Why all this celebrating?" The servant told him about the younger son coming safely home. The older son was angry because he had worked so hard for his father for many years, and the younger son had wasted everything his father had given him. But the father said to him, "Son, you are always with me, and all I have is yours. But we are happy that your brother who was lost is now found!"

Bedtime Bible Promise

Be kind and loving to each other. Forgive each other just as God forgave you in Christ.
—Ephesians 4:32

JESUS TEACHES ABOUT ENTERING THE KINGDOM OF GOD

Mark 10:13–27

The followers were upset. Many people had brought their children to Jesus so He could touch them. "Stop bringing your children!" the followers said angrily. "Jesus is too busy."

But Jesus said, "Don't stop the children from coming to Me. The kingdom of God belongs to people who are like these little children." Then Jesus gathered the children into His arms and blessed them.

As Jesus turned to leave, a man knelt down before Him. "Good teacher, what must I do to get the life that never ends?" he asked.

Jesus answered, "You must know God's commands and keep them." Then the man replied, "Teacher, I have obeyed all of God's commands since I was a boy!"

Jesus looked into his eyes. "There is still one more thing you need to do. Go and sell everything you have, and give the money to the poor. You will have a reward in heaven. Then come and follow me."

Full of sadness, the man got up and walked away. He was a very rich man, and he did not want to lose his money—not even for Jesus.

Jesus looked at His followers and said, "It is very hard for a rich person to enter the kingdom of God. It would be easier for a camel to go through the eye of a needle!"

Amazed, His followers asked, "Then who can be saved?"

Jesus answered, "This is something men cannot do. But God can do all things."

Bedtime Bible Promise

But the Lord said to me, "My grace is enough for you. When you are weak, then my power is made perfect in you."

—2 Corinthians 12:9

JESUS IS KILLED ON A CROSS

John 19–20

No matter what Pilate said, the people wanted to kill Jesus. "Take Jesus away and whip Him," Pilate ordered his soldiers. They eagerly obeyed. Then they made a crown out of thorny branches and pushed it on His head. They draped a purple robe over His shoulders and made fun of Him. "Hail, king of the Jews!" they laughed. They spit on Him and hit Him.

The religious leaders and crowd shouted, "Take Him away! Kill Him on a cross!" Then Pilate ordered Jesus to be killed.

Jesus stumbled to Golgotha. The cross He carried was very heavy. There, they nailed His hands and feet to the wood. Above His head, they nailed a sign that read, "JESUS OF NAZARETH, KING OF THE JEWS."

As Jesus hung on the cross, the soldiers decided to play a game. "Whoever wins gets to keep Jesus' clothes," they said. Everything happened just like the Bible said it would.

At last, Jesus cried out, "It is finished!" Then He bowed His head and died.

To make sure He was dead, the soldiers pierced Jesus' side with a spear. They didn't break any of His bones.

Later, Joseph of Arimathea asked Pilate, "May I take Jesus' body down for burial?" Pilate said yes. Joseph and Nicodemus wrapped Jesus' body in linen cloth with many spices and laid His body in a new tomb.

It was sad that Jesus had to die, but because of God's great love, this was not the end of the story!

THE EMPTY TOMB

John 20–21

*I*t was the first day of the week. Light from the early morning sun had just begun to shine.

Mary Magdalene was already awake. She wanted to go visit Jesus' tomb as soon as possible. But when she arrived, she became scared. "The stone has been moved away!" she gasped. Then she ran as fast as she could to tell the other followers. "They have taken the Lord out of the tomb. We don't know where they've put Him!"

Peter and another follower ran back to the tomb to see for themselves. They went inside and saw the clothes that had wrapped Jesus' body. *But where was Jesus?* they wondered. Then they hurried back to tell the others.

Meanwhile, Mary stood outside the tomb crying. Suddenly, she saw two angels sitting where Jesus' body had been. "Why are you crying?" they asked her. "They have taken away my Lord," she sobbed. As she turned around, she saw another man that she thought was the gardener.

He asked her, "Woman, why are you crying? Who are you looking for?" She answered him, "Did you take Him away, sir? Tell me where you put Him, and I will go get Him."

Then Jesus said, "Mary!" Immediately, Mary knew who He was. "Rabboni!" she rejoiced. (This means Teacher.) Jesus said, "Go back to My brothers and tell them this: 'I am going back to My Father and your Father, to My God and your God.'"

So Mary Magdalene ran back to tell Jesus' followers the incredible news. "I saw the Lord!" she shouted. And then she told them everything Jesus said.

Bedtime Bible Promise

Christ died for us while we were still sinners. In this way God shows his great love for us.

—Romans 5:8

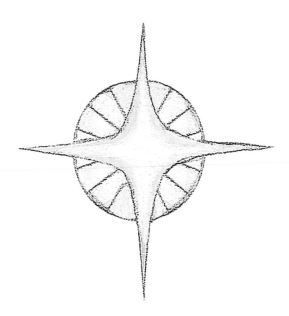

JESUS APPEARS TO THOMAS

John 20:19–29

Jesus' followers stayed close to one another inside a special locked room. They were afraid that the same people who killed Jesus would come hurt them. Suddenly, Jesus came and stood among them! "Peace be with you!" He greeted them. Then He showed them His hands and His side. They were so happy! Jesus was alive!

Thomas was not with the other followers when Jesus appeared. When his friends ran to tell him the

incredible news, Thomas thought they were lying. "I will not believe it until I put my finger where the nails were in His hands and where the spear pierced His side," Thomas answered.

A week later the followers were in the house again. This time Thomas was with them.

Again, the door was locked, but Jesus suddenly appeared inside the room with them. "Peace be with you!" Jesus announced. Then He looked at Thomas. "Come here, Thomas," Jesus called to him. "Put your finger here. Look at My hands. Put your hand here in My side. Stop doubting and believe!"

Thomas cried out, "My Lord and my God!"

Jesus answered, "You believe because you see Me. Those who believe without seeing Me will be truly happy!"

Bedtime Bible Promise

God will always give mercy to those
who worship him.
—Luke 1:50

JESUS GOES BACK TO HEAVEN

Luke 24

*M*any people had seen Jesus after He came back to life. Two men had actually walked and talked with Jesus on the road to Emmaus. They went to tell His other followers all that they had seen and heard. While everyone was standing around talking about it, Jesus Himself appeared among them.

"Peace be with you," He announced. His followers were terrified! *Is this a ghost?* they wondered. But Jesus calmed them. "Why are you afraid? Why do

you think I'm not real?" He asked as He reached toward them. "Look at My hands and feet. It's Me! Touch Me. You can see that I have a living body; a ghost does not have a body like this."

The followers were amazed and very happy. Then Jesus reminded them about the Scriptures. Even from long ago, the messages explained how Jesus would come to save lost sinners. Then Jesus helped them understand.

"Listen! My Father has promised to send you the Holy Spirit. He will help you," Jesus said. "Stay in Jerusalem until you have received that power from heaven."

Then Jesus led His followers out of Jerusalem. Outside the city, He raised His hands and blessed them. As He spoke, He was carried into heaven. "Praise Jesus, the Son of God!" His followers worshiped. After a while, they went back to Jerusalem, still excited about everything God had done. They stayed in the temple all the time and worshiped God.

Bedtime Bible Promise

And this hope will never disappoint us, because
God has poured out his love to fill our hearts.
God gave us his love through the Holy Spirit,
whom God has given to us.

—Romans 5:5

GOD'S LOVE

1 Corinthians 13:1–8

*I*magine if I could speak every language in the
world and even in heaven. It may make me sound
special and important. But if I don't have love, then
my words are just noise, like a loud bell or ringing
cymbal.

Or what if I knew all the secrets of God? Or what if
I was the smartest person around? Or maybe I had
so much faith that I could even move mountains.
Wouldn't that make me important? No, if I have all
these things but don't have love, I am nothing.

So maybe I give everything to the poor and even
give up my life. Is that the best thing I can do? No,

I get nothing by doing even these things if I don't have love.

What is love? It is patient and kind, waiting for others and helping to meet their needs. Love is not jealous, wanting what others have. It does not brag about what it does have.

It is not proud, because everything comes from God. Love is not rude, for it considers others as more important. And it does not become angry easily or remember wrongs done against it, because it is quick to forgive. Love is not happy with evil, but it is happy with the truth.

Love patiently accepts life the way it is, trusting God to do what is best. It always hopes and never gives up, because God is faithful.

Love never ends.

Bedtime Bible Promise

Dear friends, we should love each other, because love comes from God. The person who loves has become God's child and knows God.
—1 John 4:7

THE FULL ARMOR OF GOD

Ephesians 6:10–18

The Bible tells us about the armor of God. We are to be strong in the Lord—He has great power! We are to wear the full armor of God. When we wear God's armor, we will be able to fight against the Devil's evil tricks. We don't fight against people on earth. We are fighting against the rulers and authorities and powers of this world's darkness. We are fighting against spiritual powers of evil. That's why we need God's full armor. Then we will be able to stand strong

against bad things. And when the fight is over, we will still be standing.

So stand strong, with the belt of truth tied around your waist. And on your chest wear the protection of right living. On your feet wear the Good News of peace to help you stand strong. Use the shield of faith to stop the burning arrows of the Devil. Accept God's salvation as your helmet. And take the sword of the Spirit, which is the teaching of God. Pray in the Spirit at all times. Pray for everything you need. You must always be ready and never give up. Always pray for God's people.

Bedtime Bible Promise

The Lord gives strength to those who are tired.
—Isaiah 40:29

FAITH IN JESUS

1 Peter 1:3–12

Give praises to the God and Father of our Lord
Jesus Christ. God gave us great mercy and new life.
Because Jesus rose from death, God gave us a living
hope. We hope for the blessings that God has for
His children. They are kept for us in heaven, and
can't be destroyed or spoiled. God's power protects
us because we have faith in Him. He keeps us safe
until our salvation comes.

Sometimes troubles come. They help to prove
that we have faith. The purity of our faith is more
precious than gold—it will bring us praise and glory
and honor when Jesus comes again. We haven't
seen Him and we still believe in Him. Our faith

has a goal—to save our souls. We are receiving that goal, our salvation.

The prophets tried to learn about this salvation. They had the Holy Spirit with them, telling them about the troubles and sufferings that would happen. They tried to learn about it all so they could understand. They were preaching the good news of Christ to help you know the truth.

Bedtime Bible Promise

The person who trusts in himself is foolish. But the person who lives wisely will be kept safe.
—Proverbs 28:26

KING OF KINGS

Revelation 21–22

Then I saw a new heaven and a new earth. The first heaven and the first earth had disappeared. Now there was no sea. And I saw the holy city coming down out of heaven from God.

I heard a loud voice from the throne that said, "Now God's home is with men. He will live with them, and they will be His people. God Himself will be with them and will be their God. He will wipe away every tear from their eyes. There will be no more death, sadness, crying, or pain. All the old ways are gone."

The angel carried me away to a very high mountain.
He showed me the holy city, Jerusalem. It was
coming down out of heaven from God. The city
was shining with the glory of God! It was the most
beautiful thing, sparkling and dazzling like an
expensive jewel.

I did not see a temple in the holy city. The Lord
God and the Lamb are the city's temple.

The city does not need the sun or moon to shine on
it. The glory of the Lord is the city's light!

Then the angel of the Lord told me, "Listen! I am coming soon! I will bring rewards with me. I am the Alpha and the Omega, the First and the Last, the Beginning and the End."

Bedtime Bible Promise

Jesus said, "Don't let your hearts be troubled. Trust in God. And trust in me. There are many rooms in my Father's house. I would not tell you this if it were not true. I am going there to prepare a place for you."
—John 14:1-2

A PRAYER FROM SOMEONE WHO LOVES ME

_____

_____

_____

_____

_____

_____

_____

MY OWN BEDTIME PRAYER

_____

_____

_____

_____

_____

_____

_____